To Whom It May Concern
(that means you),

You've probably heard stories
about toys coming to life when
no one's watching. Maybe you
don't believe in that stuff.
But if you're reading this,
it means weird things
might have already started
happening in your house.

It usually starts with a mess you can't explain. Your parents will think you did it. You might try to blame the dog.

But it wasn't the dog.

DINOSAURS

are always hungry.

That means the kitchen is the
first place they'll go.

They'll lick all the lunch meat,
chew up the cheesy puffs,
and slobber in the salsa.

If the **DINOSAURS** find your toys, they'll want to play.

Next thing you know, they've toppled your block towers, unstuffed your sock monkey, and trashed your checkers.

Your parents probably don't let you play in the bathroom, but **DINOSAURS** aren't very good at following the rules.

The worst is when they get into your parents' stuff.

NOTHING IS SAFE
with DINOSAURS around.

Whatever you do, keep them out of the laundry room. **DINOSAURS** are

DRY

CLEAN

ONLY.

DINOSAURS

get into the most trouble while you sleep.

That scratching sound you hear late at night? It isn't a three-eyed monster or a bunch of clumsy bats.

The **DINOSAURS** are up in the attic, trying on your mom's doll clothes and getting into your dad's old comics.

Don't get

TOO

worried—

they aren't all bad.
Most people don't
know this, but some

DINOSAURS

dabble in drawing or
play Picasso with paint.

Sometimes they

GO

TOO

FAR.

Pretty soon,
you'll probably
try to stop them.
(Everybody does.)

Maybe you'll tie
them up with a
jump rope or
lock them in a
closet. When that
doesn't work,
you'll keep trying.

Don't bother—the
DINOSAURS
can get out of
ANYTHING.

ANYTHING...

The **DINOSAURS** will cause more and more trouble until they finally make a mess

SO BIG

and

SO MESSY,

you won't even be able to believe it.

Then one day you'll wake up and your house will be clean. No broken dishes, no spilled milk, no marks on the walls. A few days will pass, then a few weeks.

You'll wonder if the **DINOSAURS** will ever come out again. You might even question whether they were ever really alive to begin with, or if you made the whole thing up.

DON'T
BE
FOOLED.

That's exactly what
they want you to think.

For Adeia, Alethea, Leif, and Amarie, and their cousins, Eisley and Jude.
Also, for anyone who has ever picked up a toy and started to play or who has put
their toys away and believed they were too grown up to take them out again.

ABOUT THIS BOOK

What the Dinosaurs Did Last Night: A Very Messy Adventure was inspired by actual events—more or less. On November 1, 2012, Refe and Susan Tuma's kids woke up to discover their toy dinosaurs in the bathroom sink. The dinosaurs held toothbrushes, and toothpaste was smeared across the counter. The kids ran into their parents' room shouting, "Mom and Dad, the dinosaurs came to life last night, and we caught them brushing their teeth!" They asked whether the dinosaurs would do it again. Refe and Susan, seeing their kids' delight, answered with an enthusiastic "Yes!"

For the next twenty-nine days, the kids woke up each morning and searched for what the dinosaurs had done the night before. Refe and Susan began documenting their dinosaurs' nightly mischief in 2012 under the name Dinovember. Since then, families in more than fifty countries have reported dinosaur activity, and Dinovember has grown to become an international celebration of childhood imagination and wonder and a reminder that no one is ever too old to play.

This book was edited by Mary-Kate Gaudet and designed by Phil Caminiti under the art direction of Dave Caplan. The production was supervised by Erika Schwartz, and the production editor was Barbara Bakowski. The text was set in Franklin Gothic and display type was set in Franklin Gothic Hand Demi and hand-lettered.

The photographs in this book were taken using a digital SLR camera with a 24-70mm lens and a custom bacon modification designed to attract hungry dinosaurs. All but two interior photographs were taken inside Refe and Susan's house (because you do NOT want to see their actual laundry room). No dinosaurs were harmed in the making of this book, with the exception of Vincent the *Dilophosaurus*. He was treated with high-quality superglue and has since made a full recovery.

• Little, Brown and Company • Hachette Book Group • 1290 Avenue of the Americas, New York, NY 10104 • Visit us at lb-kids.com • Little, Brown and Company is a division of Hachette Book Group, Inc. The Little, Brown name and logo are trademarks of Hachette Book Group, Inc. • The publisher is not responsible for websites (or their content) that are not owned by the publisher. • First Edition: October 2015 • Library of Congress Cataloging-in-Publication Data • Tuma, Refe. What the dinosaurs did last night: a very messy adventure/ by Refe and Susan Tuma.—First edition. • pages cm • Summary: Photographs and simple text reveal the mischief toy dinosaurs get into all night long, from knocking over potted plants to painting on walls. • ISBN 978-0-316-33562-1 (hardcover : alk. paper) [1. Dinosaurs—Fiction. 2. Toys—Fiction. 3. Behavior—Fiction. 4. Humorous stories.] I. Tuma, Susan. II. Title. • PZ7.1.T86Wh 2015 • [E]—dc23 • 2014031338 • 10 9 8 7 6 • PHX
PRINTED IN THE UNITED STATES OF AMERICA